Book Four

of the

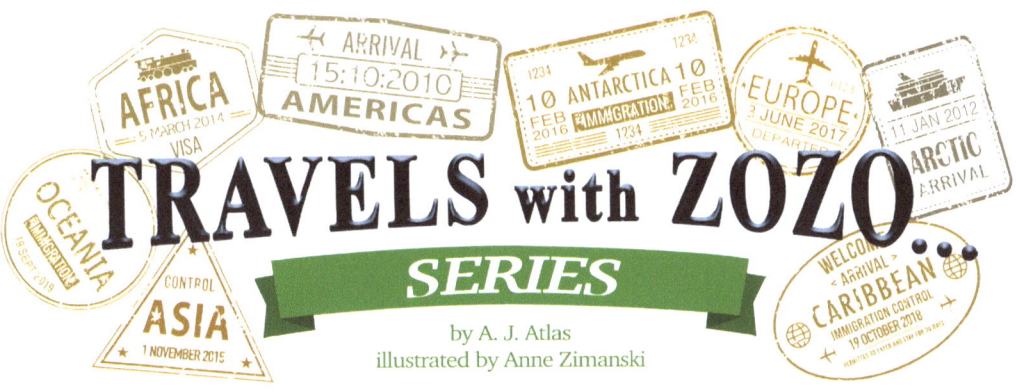

by A. J. Atlas
illustrated by Anne Zimanski

Welcome, Readers!

Before you get started, I thought you might like to know a few interesting things about the *Travels with Zozo...*™ series. First of all, the stories are set in real places, so the illustrations you'll see try to show the actual landscapes, plants, and animals found in those locations. Second, the cultural and historical elements you'll read about are also as accurate as possible. I hope this knowledge makes the books even more enjoyable for you.

For this story, the settings are Incahuasi Island, the Salar de Uyuni, Tunupa Volcano, and Eduardo Avaroa National Reserve in the South American country of Bolivia.

In a few parts of the story, a teeny bit more creativity and imagination was added. Most of it will be quite obvious, like viscachas doing yoga! Other, less obvious, elements that are not 100% accurate include the following:

- The lizards pictured live in Bolivia, but only along the edges of the salt flat.
- The flowers on the cactuses on Incahuasi Island bloom white, not pink.
- Flamingos and viscachas should not be approached, even though Zozo does. It is not safe to go near or try to touch unknown animals.

For the most part, the rest of the information I have presented is accurate and, in my opinion, super interesting! Here are a few more fun facts:

- Aymara and Quechua are the names of local indigenous languages in Bolivia.
- Approximately 30,000 to 40,000 years ago, the salt flat, called the Salar de Uyuni, was part of a giant, prehistoric, inland sea called Lake Minchin. Two modern lakes, Lake Titicaca and Lake Poopo, were also part of Lake Minchin. During the rainy season, the modern lakes overflow and flood the salt flat. When the flooding occurs, the water creates a mirror effect, leading the Salar to be called the largest mirror in the world!
- A giant hummingbird is about the same size as a starling or cardinal, 9 inches (23 cm) long.
- The salt flat's polygonal shapes initially form from below. In the fluid (water, salt, minerals, dirt, etc.) below the surface, a convection cell creates a flow of lighter fluid rising and heavier fluid sinking. The repeated rising imprints a geometric pattern on the layers of the crust as it dries. Then the heat of the sun, high altitude, and low humidity combine to rapidly dry out layers, and cracks form along the lines of the imprinted shapes. Finally, air pressure and low-level humidity act like straws to suck up fluid and salt through the cracks, forming raised mounds of salt along the cracks.
- Infinite perspective photography is possible when a flat, unbroken landscape gives a person's eye no visual reference point to put objects into perspective. This allows the eyes to be tricked into seeing things as much smaller, or larger, than they actually are.

— AJA

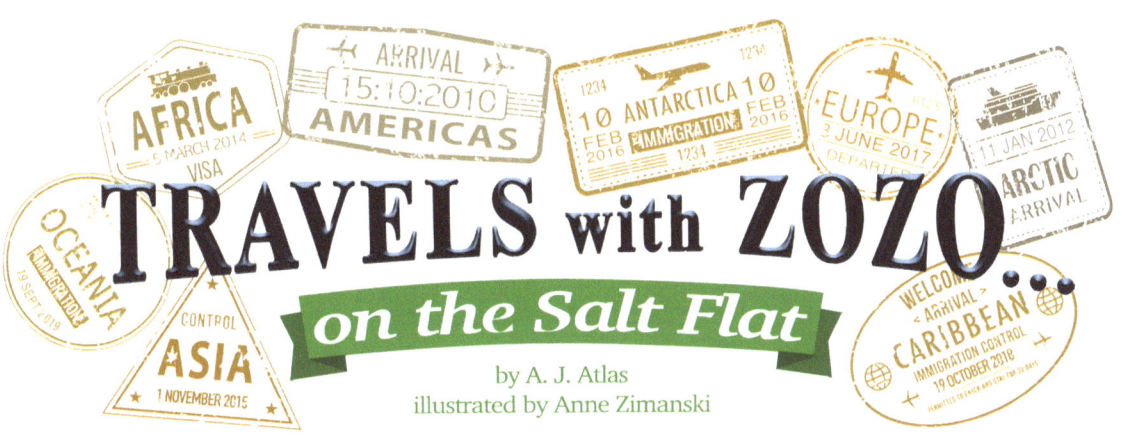

TRAVELS with ZOZO...
on the Salt Flat

by A. J. Atlas
illustrated by Anne Zimanski

IMAGINON BOOKS

Zozo was a hoppity, floppity, huggable, snuggable pet bunny who loved to sleep.

She lived with a fun, on-the-run family of four who **loved** to travel. Together, they crisscrossed the world sharing adventures and making new friends.

Often, Zozo slept surrounded by small noises. *Tick-tick-tick. Rumble-rumble-rumble. Rat-a-tat-tat.* Sometimes, the soft sounds even helped soothe her to sleep.

This time, however, it was entirely different! As the little truck rumbled over the rocks, along the gravelly ruts, it was far **too bumpy** and **too noisy** to sleep. Seatbelts jangled. Doors rattled. Windows whistled, and overhead luggage clattered about in the strong wind.

This wildly beautiful place was like nowhere Zozo had ever been. She could see snowcapped volcanoes in the distance. Steam rose up through holes in the ground, and animals played everywhere. The topsy-turvy ride through it all just made it even more fun.

Hours later, Zozo edged closer to the window and a view that had changed dramatically. The ground was brilliantly white and perfectly flat. Curious cracks were everywhere, creating all kinds of interconnected shapes.

It looks like, well, um...a giant puzzle? What type of ground makes puzzle-piece shapes? she asked herself.

Soon, Zozo got the chance to find out. The truck stopped in the middle of the vast, white plain, in front of a cactus-studded patch of land. Everyone went outside.

"Explore the island all you like," Dad said to the entire family. "You can't get lost. Just watch for us when it's time to leave."

Island? Zozo questioned while scratching her head with her back foot. Two times before, she had been on an island, and water had surrounded them. *If this is an island, then where is the water?* she wondered.

Determined to find answers to her questions, Zozo scampered onto the mysterious island. *Hop, hop, hop.* Up the steep, rocky hill, she climbed higher to get a better look around.

Suddenly, Zozo ducked as two flamingos swooped down from overhead. They zigzagged between flowering cactuses, taking turns leading, until the two flew around a boulder and out of sight.

Then Zozo heard *skrrreeek*—a loud scrape—and *kuuu, kuuu, kachunk*—the sound of rocks falling. *Uh oh!* Zozo worried.

"Help!" came a voice from above her.

Zozo scurried toward the sound.

"Help!" she heard again.

Zozo arrived at a natural rock arch. There, she saw the two flamingos again. One bird had a leg trapped under a fallen rock wall, and the other was hopping around calling for help.

"I can help," Zozo offered. "Are you hurt?"

"I'm fine," said the hopping flamingo. "But my brother, Quechua, might be hurt."

"I'm just stuck, Aymara, not hurt," the grounded flamingo said, looking at the large pile of rocks on top of his webbed foot. He turned toward Zozo and said, "I would love your help."

Zozo quickly got to work. "You'll be out soon, Quechua," she assured him. "By the way, I'm Zozo."

Zozo carefully lifted rocks from the top of the pile and carried them off to the side. Aymara tried to help, but her wings were not as good at grasping rocks as Zozo's paws were. Instead, she used her feathers to sweep away pebbles.

Zozo stopped a moment to catch her breath. The biggest rocks still remained on top of Quechua's foot. But she was hot. She wished she had some water, which reminded her of the mystery of the island. "Is there water around here?" she asked the flamingos.

"Sort of," Quechua said, still unable to free his leg. He gestured toward the wide-open, white plain with his wing and began to explain.

"Here in Bolivia, you could have had all the water you wanted...tens of thousands of years ago!" Quechua giggled. "Back then, this was a great inland sea with water in every direction. Can you imagine that? Fish swam in the water, birds flew all around, and this island was part of a coral reef."

"Where did the water go?" Zozo asked.

Aymara leaned in and answered, "The water on the surface dried up. It left salt from the seawater to form this salty, white crust. And the reef turned to rock."

Zozo inspected the coral rock Aymara was looking at before lifting it away from Quechua's foot. Then Zozo gazed out at the wave-shaped, dried salt along the shoreline, closed her eyes, and imagined all the white salt was blue water. It made sense. She opened her eyes, amazed.

"*¡Excelente! Mis amigos,*" said a furry animal rapidly approaching the group. Then, switching from Spanish to English, he continued, "My friends, let me help you, and I can practice my English too."

"Oh, a viscacha to the rescue! Bolivia's most helpful friend!" Quechua remarked, turning to meet the bunny-squirrel-like creature with a smile and a nod.

Immediately, the viscacha grabbed the other end of a heavy rock Zozo was lifting and helped Zozo move it. "My name is Bisi," he said, reaching for another large rock to clear away.

"Nice to meet you, Bisi," Zozo said before Aymara, Quechua, and Zozo introduced themselves.

With the large rocks now gone, Quechua slipped his leg out of the rubble and stood. Unhurt, he took a few steps. "Thank you!" he gushed. "How can I ever repay you for helping me?"

"Could we fly with you?" Bisi suggested eagerly.

"A ride through the cactuses would be fun," Zozo agreed, eyeing the hillside obstacle course with a big grin.

"Our pleasure!" the flamingos said together.

Bisi climbed up on Quechua, and Zozo hopped up on Aymara.

The flamingos lifted off into the sky. First, they flew through the cactus forest, in and out, around and around, with Bisi and Zozo squealing with joy. Then they glided in great circles above the salt flat. Zozo could see the entire coral island surrounded by the sea of white salt.

"This is the biggest salt flat in the world! It's bigger than some countries!" Aymara said with a powerful flap of her wings. "Would you like to see more?"

Zozo and Bisi nodded yes.

Side-by-side, in the wide-open sky, the flamingos covered a large distance in a short time. Soon, Zozo could see a flooded area of the salt flat. "Finally, I see water!" Zozo announced as the flamingos descended toward the shiny, reflective pool.

The flamingos landed and walked for a few minutes in the mirror-like, shallow water before beginning their return flight to the island.

"**Amazing**!" Bisi and Zozo said at the same time.

Once they were back on the island, Zozo gave her new friends a hug goodbye. A chorus of "thank yous" chimed from the group before Zozo turned and headed toward her family. They had finished exploring the island and were all together on the salt flat taking pictures.

As soon as Zozo hopped off the island and onto the cool, damp ground, she had an idea. *Sniff, sniff, sniff.* Zozo smelled the white puzzle piece beneath her paws and then cautiously licked it. *Sure enough, Aymara was right! It is salt!* she thought.

Pleased with herself for learning the mysteries of Bolivia's island in the salt flat, Zozo joined her family's photo shoot.

Zozo didn't understand how the photos looked so goofy. But she was too tired to think about it. *That mystery will have to wait for another day,* she sighed. Then she smiled and struck a silly pose.

Discover Zambia's great waterfall in Zozo's next adventure, *Travels with Zozo... under the Moonbow!*

Travels with Zozo...on the Salt Flat   by A.J. Atlas   illustrated by Anne Zimanski

Published by ImaginOn Books, an imprint of ImaginOn LLC
www.imaginonbooks.com

Copyright © 2022 by A.J. Atlas

All rights reserved. No part of this book, in whole or in part, may be reproduced, scanned, recorded, photocopied, photographed, transmitted in any form or by any means, broadcast, distributed in any printed, mechanical, or electronic form, or stored by any information storage and retrieval system now known or hereafter invented, **without the prior written permission of the publisher and copyright owners,** except for the inclusion of brief quotations embodied in acknowledged articles or reviews.

1st Edition
2 4 6 8 10 9 7 5 3 1

978-1-954405-04-2 (Hardcover)   978-1-954405-34-9 (Ebook)

Printed in U.S.A.

To purchase books or obtain more information about the author, illustrator, or upcoming books, visit www.travelswithzozo.com

CPSIA information can be obtained
at www.ICGtesting.com
Printed in the USA
LVHW050230301021
701739LV00004B/31